This igloo book belongs to:

....

iglobooks

igloobooks

Published in 2020
by Igloo Books Ltd
Cottage Farm
Sywell
NN6 0BJ
www.igloobooks.com

0820 001
2 4 6 8 10 9 7 5 3 1
ISBN 978-1-83903-314-8

Written by Stephanie Moss
Illustrated by Chiara Galletti

Designed by Justine Ablett
Edited by Stephanie Moss

Printed and manufactured in China

ROCKIN' REINDEER

igloobooks

Everyone felt jolly because
Christmas time was here.
All except the reindeer,
who were quite grumpy this year.

They used to be best friends with Santa.
Now something was wrong.
The fame had got too much and he
read fan mail all day long!

"Why should HE be famous? WE'RE the ones who pull his sleigh!
Until Santa says sorry," they said, "we'll be on our way."

They slammed the door behind them and said, **"Now what shall we do?"**
So, they set off to do something that would make them stand out, too.

After a little while, there came a rocking music sound.
"What's that?" a polar bear said, as he looked all around.

POW-WOW went the guitar.
A drum went BANG-BANG-BANG!
WAH-WAH went the bass...
... and fa-la-oo the singer sang.

"It's you! You're Santa's reindeer,"
the polar bear called out.
"One day you'll all be famous!
I haven't any doubt."

"Come on, Rockin' Reindeer.
I'm taking you on tour.
You won't be pulling Santa in
his red sleigh any more!"

AND SO THE ROCKIN' REINDEER WERE AN OVERNIGHT SENSATION!

The stadiums were packed and they performed in every nation.

They flew on private jets and all their pictures were online.
When Santa heard the news he cried out,

So Santa held auditions
to replace his reindeer crew.
Creatures of all kinds turned up
to see if they'd get through.

He said

NO!

to a dragon,
when he breathed
fire in the sky.

Unicorns weren't Christmassy...

... and narwhals couldn't fly!

That night, Mrs Claus made Santa a nice cup of tea.
"There's no team like your reindeer," she said.
"Wouldn't you agree?"

So he called a dear old friend.
It was the polar bear!

Please help me get them back,

he said,

to show how much I care.

The polar bear agreed and he arranged a special show. **"Your North Pole concert is sold out,"** he told them. **"Quick, let's go!"**

Suddenly, backstage, Santa
appeared before their eyes.
He told them he'd arranged the
show as a Christmas surprise.

"No one else can pull the
sleigh quite like all of you can.
But I want to tell you something," he said.

... I'M YOUR BIGGEST FAN!

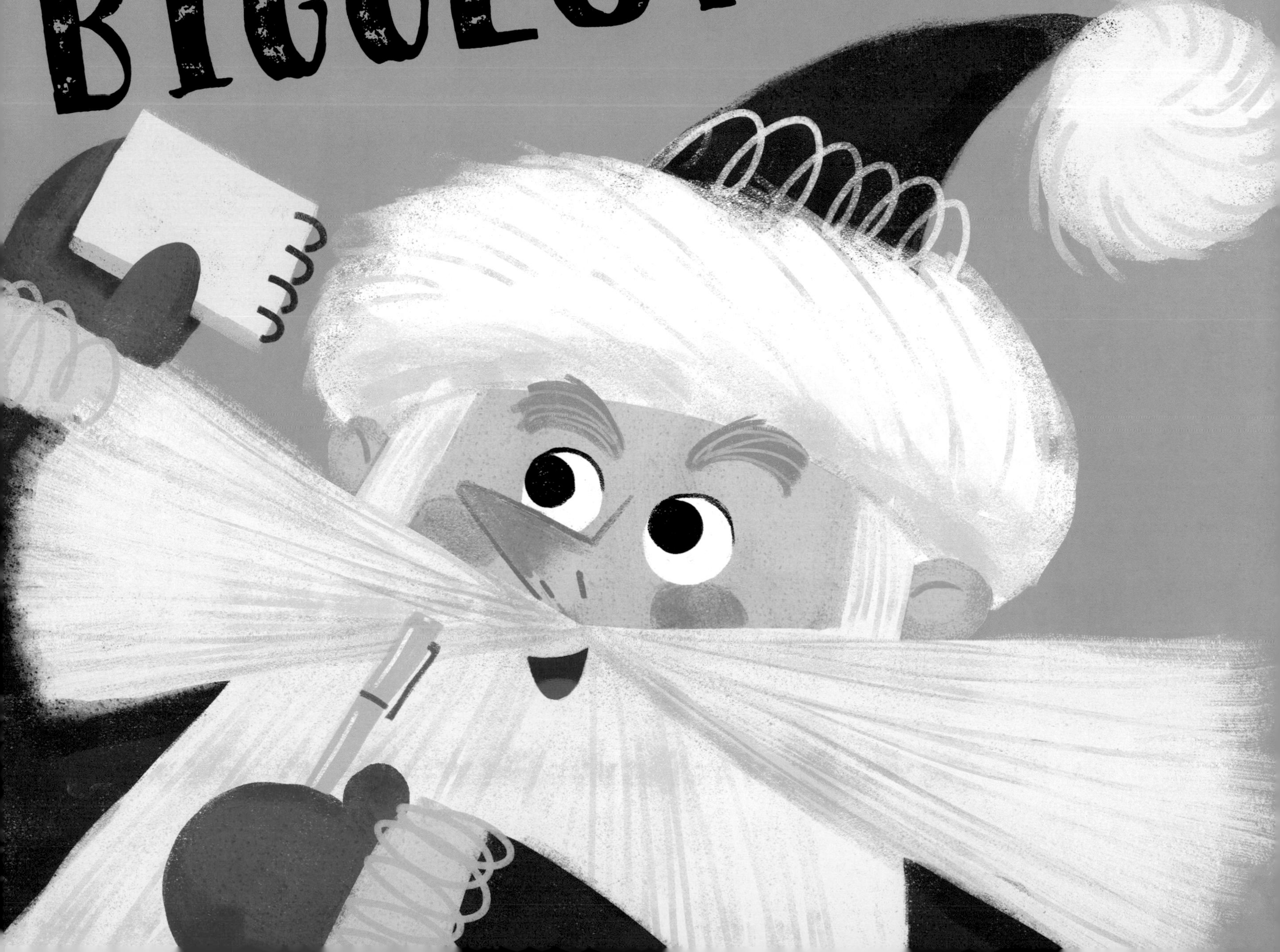

The reindeer were so pleased. It's what they'd wanted all along.
"We've missed you," they said. **"So this will be our final song."**

And so, after their encore, they took off into the sky.
"Have a Rockin' Christmas! Goodnight, everyone. Goodbye!"